So... What Col Were the Dinosaurs, Anyway?

By Denise M. Oliansky

Illustrated by Carla P. Hood

The author and illustrator are sisters, and this is their first children's book.

The author, Denise Oliansky, lives in Michigan. She has a Master's degree in developmental psychology and works in health services research. She enjoys writing poetry and prose and is currently working on her first mystery novel.

Carla Hood, the illustrator, is a registered nurse living in Latham, New York, with her husband, and two children. She has a talent and passion for crafting, particularly for those projects involving diverse painting techniques.

Published by Parlance Press
14709 Longtin
Southgate, MI 48195
www.parlancepress.com
doliansky@parlancepress.com

Oliansky, Denise M.
    So...what color were the dinosaurs, anyway? / Denise M. Oliansky, Carla P. Hood.
    Southgate, MI : Parlance Press, 2002.

        p. ; cm.

    SUMMARY: An imaginative portrayal of dinosaurs in the colors of modern-day birds. A poetry, illustration and coloring book all in one.
    ISBN: 0-9710952-0-5

    1. Dinosaurs – Juvenile fiction. 2. Dinosaurs – Fiction. I. Hood, Carla P. II.
    Title. III. So...what color were the dinosaurs, anyway?

PZ7.0453	2002	2001094457
So 2002	-dc21	CIP

PROJECT COORDINATION BY JENKINS GROUP, INC.

06 05 04 03 02 ✳ 6 5 4 3 2

Proudly printed in the United States of America

This book is dedicated to
Henry and Adele Muczenski,
our wonderful parents,
in gratitude for their constant
love, support, and encouragement
throughout our lives.
—*D.O. & C.H.*

In most dinosaur books that you open
you'll see dinosaurs colored dull gray,
roaming through thick green forests
on a sunny, blue-skyed day...

Who is to say what color they were,
since they lived such a long time ago.
All we have left are
some old white bones,
so there's really no
way to know...

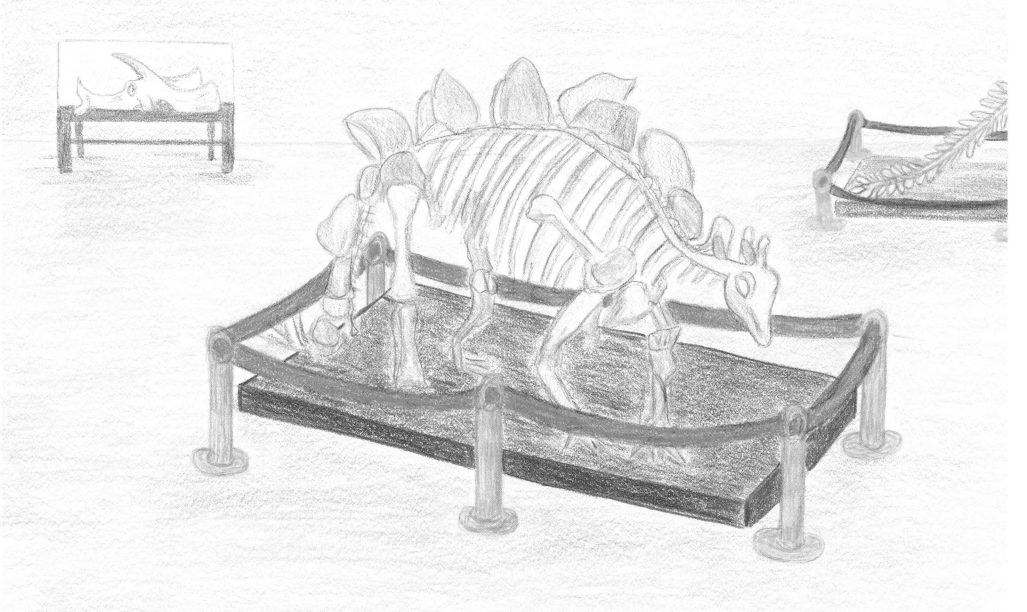

But, some scientists say the dinosaurs
might have led to the birds we now see.
If they were the colors
we see on our birds,
just imagine how splendid they'd be!...

Stegosaurus would be quite a treat
brightly streaked
like a Parakeet...

Stegosaurus
(steg-uh-SORE-us)

Spotting him would be a cinch
if Triceratops glowed
like a Yellow Finch...

Triceratops
(try-SER-uh-tops)

Wouldn't Diplodocus look absurd with the ruby throat of the Hummingbird?...

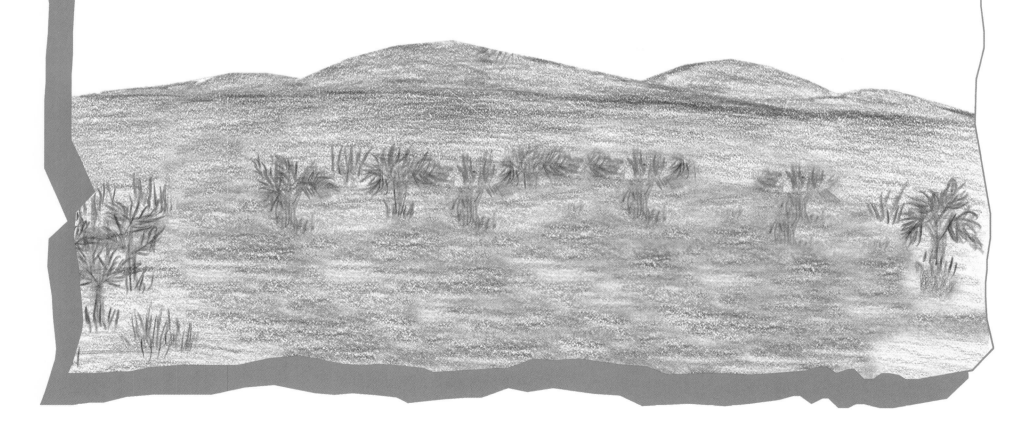

Diplodocus
(dih-PLOD-uh-kus)

Tyrannosaurus Rex
looks a lot less rotten
with the red-orange breast of
a sweet little Robin...

Tyrannosaurus
Rex
(ty-ran-us-SORE-us)

Very much like a bird is the
Velociraptor
the red of the Cardinal
is the color we're after...

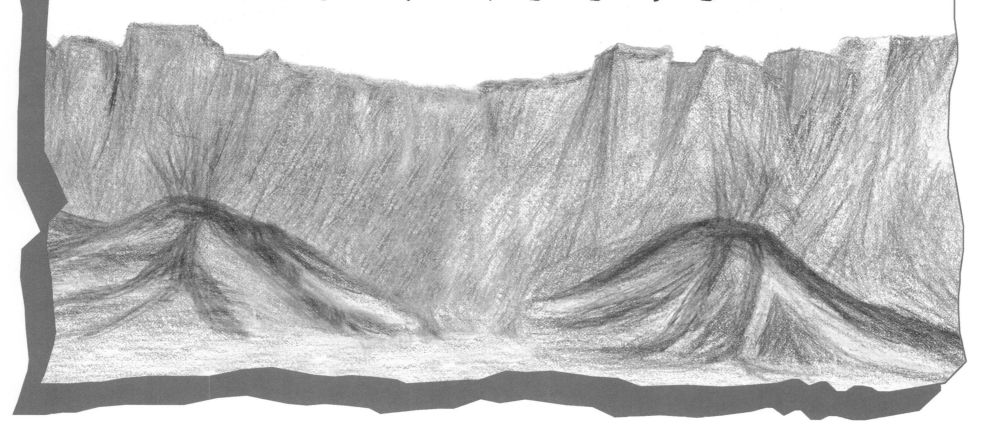

Velociraptor
(vel-os-ih-RAPT-or)

Psittacosaurus
with its beak like a **Parrot**
whatever the color...
this dino could wear it!

Psittacosaurus
(si-tack-oh-SORE-us)

Megalosaurus would be
rather pleasant
all speckled and spotted like a
Ringnecked Pheasant...

Megalosaurus

(meg-ah-lo-SORE-us)

And the winged Pterodactyl
is flying your way
dressed up and screeching
like a noisy **Bluejay**...

Pterodactyl
(ter-oh-DAKT-il)

Now here's some more dinos
with no color at all.
They are in need
of some beautiful hues.
So grab your crayons
and think of some birds,
and color each one
any way that you choose!...

Brontosaurus
(bront-oh-SAWR-us)

Coelophysis
(see-lo-FISE-iss)

Dimetrodon
(dye-met-RO-don)

Hadrosaurs
(HAD-ruh-sorz)

Parasaurolophus
(par-ah-SAWR-ol-uh-fus)

Struthiomimus
(strooth-ee-uh-MY-mus)